Before I Wake Up…

Britta Teckentrup

Prestel   Munich · London · New York

Before I wake up,
I float through my dreams ...
imagining worlds.
Never ending it seems.

Before I wake up,

I fly into the night.

I gaze at the stars,

the moon shining bright.

In the blue meadow,

I'm joined by my friend.

We travel together

in our world without end.

Together we fly

with arms stretched out wide

over the seas

and leave our worries behind.

Before I wake up,

we might face some storms.

But I won't be afraid.

I'm safe in your arms.

We feel the wind.

We hear the sea.

We sing our song.

Together we're strong.

Before I wake up,

we sail through the seas.

Our boat rocking gently

in the soft breeze.

I swim with the whales…

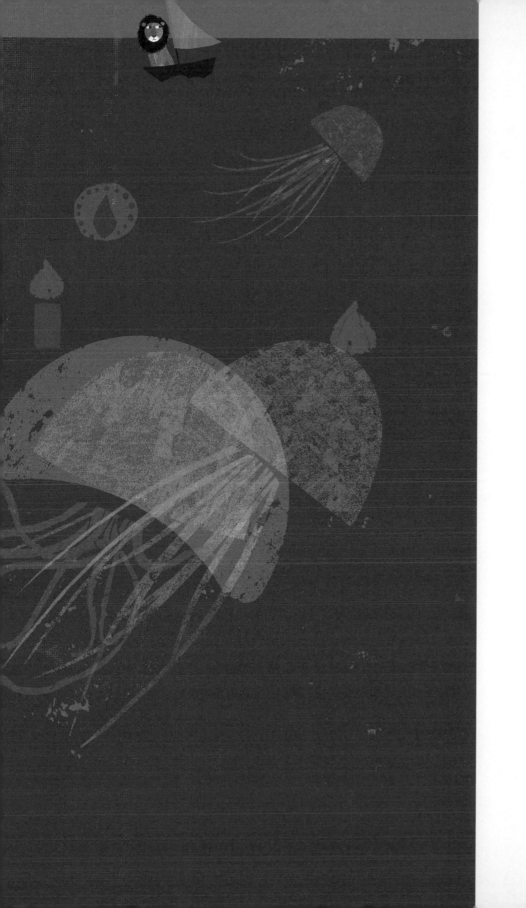

I dive into the ocean ...

I close my eyes,

so full of emotion.

When I open my eyes,
we're deep in a wood.
We follow the path.
I feel so good.

We meet wild creatures,

surrounded by trees.

They say, "Happy to meet you!

Will you stay with us, please?"

We play through the night,

and I have to confess

that I wish I could stay

in this wilderness.

You make me feel safe,

you are always near.

That's why I am brave,

without any fear…

But the time has come,
as night fades away,
to leave our new friends
and welcome the day.

We run faster and faster

out of the night...

through the red jungle...

toward morning's light.

And when the day dawns,
I stand close to my friend.
"Goodbye for now!"
Night has come to an end.

When I wake up,

the sun kisses my skin.

It's a wonderful world.

Let the new day begin!

For the child in you …

© Prestel Verlag, Munich · London · New York, 2016

Prestel, Munich
A member of Verlagsgruppe Random House GmbH

Prestel Verlag
www.prestel.de

Prestel Publishing Ltd.
14-17 Wells Street
London W1T 3PD

Prestel Publishing
900 Broadway, Suite 603
New York, NY 10003

www.prestel.com

Library of Congress Control Number is available;
British Library Cataloguing-in-Publication Data: a catalogue
record for this book is available from the British Library.

Editorial direction: Doris Kutschbach
Copyediting: Rita Forbes and Brad Finger
Production: Astrid Wedemeyer
Typesetting: Meike Sellier
Origination: ReproLine mediateam, Munich
Printing and binding: DZS Grafik, d.o.o., Ljublijana

Verlagsgruppe Random House FSC® N001967
The FSC®-certified paper *Tauro* has been
supplied by Igepa, Germany

ISBN 978-3-7913-7246-4